Creative Girls
Enchanted
Adventures

Adventure Book 2

The Emerald Dragon

Annie's®
AnniesCraftStore.com

The Emerald Dragon
Copyright © 2014 Annie's.

Library of Congress-in-Publication Data
The Emerald Dragon / by Jan Fields
p. cm.
I. Title

2014951058

AnniesCraftStore.com
(800) 282-6643
Creative Girls Enchanted Adventures™
Series Editors: Shari Lohner, Janice Tate, and Ken Tate
Cover Illustrator: Kelley McMorris

10 11 12 13 14 | Printed in USA | 9 8 7 6 5 4 3 2

PROLOGUE

One summer day in the woody hills of Portal, Connecticut, the six creative and adventurous girls of Stone Hollow Lane all received a mysterious package in the mail. Each package contained one oddly heavy, triangle-shaped medallion engraved with a design. The girls had no idea who sent the medallions or why—or that their lives were about to get *very* exciting. They met at the neighborhood clubhouse and discovered that when placed together, the medallions opened a secret doorway to a magical world called the Realm.

Ever curious, they entered the Realm … and that's when their first grand adventure began! The girls were met by a magical creature who informed them they were the lost princesses of this extraordinary world. Even more surprising, each girl discovered she possessed an amazing magical power tied to her unique creative talents and imagination. The girls haven't *quite* mastered those newfound powers yet, and sometimes this lands them in a bit of trouble ....

CHAPTER ONE
The Invitation

Shaylee scooped up the notebook and her favorite purple pen with the fluffy feathers on top. She sat cross-legged on her bed and stared at the smooth blank page of the notebook. "I can't believe I have homework and school hasn't even started yet," she grumbled. It wasn't really homework, of course. It was really her friend Rissa's idea that she and her five friends each write down what happened when they all saved the Wellspring of Magic.

Then she wrote:

"It began with the strange packages. We each got one. I mean me, Shaylee; plus Alysa and Rachel, who are twins; and Kaida, Marisol, and Larissa. Only we don't ever call Alysa or Larissa by their real names because they sound so much alike. We call them Aly and Rissa."

Shaylee frowned and scribbled out the part about the names, muttering, "That's goofy. We know what our names are."

Then she took a deep breath and went on writing.

"Inside each package was a magnet thing with a picture on it. We didn't know they were magical keys to a different world until later."

Shaylee stared at the paragraph. That's not really when it started, she realized. It started when all the houses in their neighborhood sold at the same time, and all to families with girls about the same age. She scribbled that down, and then stopped. Maybe it didn't really start then. Maybe it started when the girls met and found the funny park in the middle of the neighborhood.

"The park was full of weeds and bugs and statues of people that no one knew. We made a clubhouse in an old building at the middle of the park. We still go there almost every day to hang out and do crafts and talk about Wellspring. That's where Rissa said we should all write down what happened, so we'll have a record. Sometimes Rissa is a little bossy."

Shaylee tickled her nose with the pen's feathers as she stopped and thought. Then she scratched out the last sentence a bunch of times. "I should stick to the adventure part," she muttered. She took a deep breath and wrote really fast.

"The magnet things make some kind of hole when we stick them together. We used the hole to go into a different world that we call Wellspring, but the people there just call it 'the Realm' which sounds kind of old-fashioned to me. When we're there, we're all princesses, and we can do magic."

Shaylee stopped again and wondered if she should add that they couldn't do the magic very well most of the time. Then she sighed. "Just write fast and get it over with," she told herself.

"When we're in this magic world, we're all good at different things. I had to do a special dance to bring the magic water back to the fountain, the Wellspring of Magic. But first we had to go on this huge quest, and everybody had to work together. Rachel talks to animals, Aly talks to plants, Rissa can turn her poems into magic spells, Marisol can turn into a mermaid, and Kaida is just more Kaida than ever. She can start fires by just thinking about it, which was really helpful when we were all dripping wet and cold.

"Anyway, while we were there, we met these bears who could turn into people, but they were stuck being bears until we fixed the Wellspring. We also met people who made magical jewelry, and they gave each of us a special bead. We even met a dragon who lived in a river and almost drowned me. It turned out that he was nice, just a little scary at first.

"The magic that was left in the Realm before we fixed the Wellspring of Magic was changing, going bad. We saw plants that drank blood, and I had to help save one of the Guardian bears from the vampire plants because only I was small enough. That was scary, but not as scary as fighting giant spiders at the fountain. So even though we had to do a lot of stuff, we fixed the Wellspring of Magic and were able to come home again. We're thinking we'll go back soon, but I don't know when."

Shaylee stared at her notebook and sighed. She sure hoped everyone else wrote better reports than she did. "Maybe I should write more about the dancing part," she muttered.

Shaylee jumped when she heard a sharp rap at the door just before it flew open. Rissa burst in, and Shaylee gawked at her.

"Your hair is pink!" Shaylee exclaimed. Rissa's chin-length hair was a soft cotton-candy pink.

"The temporary red from yesterday didn't wash all the way out," Rissa said.

"It's pretty."

"You just say that because it matches your …" Rissa paused and glanced around the room, "everything."

Shaylee's room was decorated in shades of pink with a few green accent pieces. Rissa turned in a slow circle as she looked at everything. "Wow," she said, "your room looks like the inside of someone's nose!"

"Ewww, thanks," Shaylee said. "If I wanted to hear gross stuff about my room, I could ask my brothers. Did you want something?"

"Oh, right. There's an emergency meeting at the clubhouse."

Shaylee looked at her friend nervously. She figured the girls were getting anxious to go back to the magical world, but Shaylee was in no hurry. It was cool to be able to do magic, but their last adventure was really scary. Finally, she sighed and asked, "Why?"

"Have you looked at your Realm key lately?" Rissa asked.

Shaylee shook her head as she hopped up off her bed. "I've been doing clubhouse *homework*." She walked over to her small pink-and-white desk and pulled open the drawer.

A soft light pulsed from inside the drawer. Shaylee picked up her glowing Realm key.

As she held the quarter-sized triangle of metal in her hand, the glow brightened, and an image appeared in the air over the key. It looked like a square envelope with a thick wax seal on the flap. The seal was stamped with the same figure of the dancing fairy that was on Shaylee's Realm key.

As Shaylee watched, the seal broke and the envelope opened. A card slipped out and hung in the air in the light of the Realm key. The print on the card was fancy, and Shaylee squinted to make out the words:

> *Official Invitation to the*
> *Celebration of Gratitude and Joy*
> *Honoring the return of Wellspring*
> *And the Courage of the Six Princesses of the Realm*
> *In the Village of the Meadow Folk*
> *On the last day of the Feast Cycle*

"When's the last day of the Feast Cycle?" she asked.

"We don't know," Rissa said. "That's why we're having the meeting."

Shaylee closed her hand over the glowing Realm key, and the image of the invitation vanished. She slipped the key into the pocket of her pink skinny jeans and grinned at her friend. "I love parties. They're way more fun than giant spiders and vampire plants. Let's go!"

As Rissa and Shaylee walked between the strange statues in the park to reach the clubhouse, Shaylee kept her eyes down. Normally she liked statues, but these gave her the creeps. They all looked angry. Who would fill a park full of grumpy marble people? Their neighborhood was full of weird mysteries like that.

When they walked into the old stone building they used for a clubhouse, Kaida was leaning against the table where they did their crafts. She looked up as soon as they stepped inside and said, "Great, we can get started."

"Started doing what?" Shaylee asked.

"Since we don't know what the Feast Cycle is," Aly answered, "we thought we'd go into the Realm and ask."

"We don't want to miss the party," Marisol added. She stood and danced with her hands in the air. "I love parties."

"Me too," Shaylee agreed, though she had hoped they'd have a little more time to get used to the idea of jumping back into the magical land. It did make sense to check on the date though. "Should we put the keys on the table like last time?"

Kaida shook her head. "It was too hard climbing down into the hole. I think we should try putting them on the wall. They could make something more like a window."

The girls gathered around a flat expanse of wall. "Do you think they'll stick?" Shaylee asked.

"They do," Aly said, putting her key with its delicate flower and vine design on the wall. "We already tried."

Rachel pressed her key with the bear on it to the wall

near her twin sister's. The two keys snapped together. "If it opens back into the forest, we can ask Fleet about the date," Rachel said.

Shaylee glanced at her friend and noticed Rachel's pink cheeks. She suspected Rachel had a crush on Fleet—at least when he was in his cute guy form.

Rissa added her key with the open book design. She whispered, "Rachel's got a boyfriend."

Rachel gave her a friendly shove and laughed. "We're just friends."

"Sure," Kaida said, as her flying unicorn key snapped into place. "We totally believe you."

"Totally," added Marisol, pressing her key into place. The river dragon on the key seemed to glow brighter as the keys united.

Then the girls turned to Shaylee. The younger girl held her key tightly in her hand. "Everything will be OK," she told herself. Then she stepped forward and slipped her key into place with shaky fingers. "I just hope we can stay away from spiders this time."

The keys made a tight ring on the wall, and the small circle of rock in the middle seemed to disappear as if the girls could see through to the outside. Then the keys slid apart slightly, and the hole grew bigger. A thin, green face popped up into the empty space, and Shaylee shrieked.

"It's about time!" the frowning man snapped. "We have much to do." He reached up and stretched the hole until his upper body showed clearly. He was dressed in a fancy white shirt and a green vest heavily embroidered with brightly colored flowers and vines.

"Who are you?" Kaida asked, frowning.

"I am Thornspinner Flax Martinsong," he said. "It is my job to help you princesses prepare for the celebration. I am the director of protocol and decorum. We understand that even though you are princesses, you have grown up in a barbaric world and aren't likely to know how to behave in proper company."

"Don't know how to behave?" Kaida echoed, frowning. "There is nothing wrong with our manners." Then she looked at Rissa, who was grinning. "Well, maybe Rissa could use some work, but the rest of us do just fine."

"I went to my cousin's wedding," Marisol added. "It was very fancy, so I learned all about proper manners."

Shaylee had actually read a couple of books on manners, so she thought she was probably OK on most things, but she still wouldn't mind listening just to be sure. "It would be OK to get a few tips," she said. She turned toward the man in the wall. "When is the celebration?"

"The last day of the Feast Cycle, of course," the thin man said, speaking as if Shaylee was unusually stupid. "Didn't you princesses read your invitations?"

"When is the last day of the Feast Cycle?" Kaida asked. Her voice was very quiet, and her friends knew that meant she was getting really mad. The fussy man must have sensed it because he took a small step away from the hole.

"Tomorrow," he said. "It begins early."

14

"Then you better just hit the high points on the manners stuff," Rissa suggested. "What do we have to know?"

"Well, your clothes will be taken care of after you arrive. Do try to do something nice with your hair," he said, looking pointedly at Rissa. "And we should go through gift protocol."

"We get gifts?" Shaylee said, delighted at the idea of more magical gifts.

"Get and give," the man responded, and again he seemed to think the question ridiculous. "It's a *gratitude* celebration." He glanced from girl to girl, clearly expecting that to be meaningful. Then he shook his head sadly. "Everyone will bring a gift. It should be wrapped. Make certain the wrapping reflects something about you as the giver. And the gift must be something you have made."

"But we just found out about it today!" Kaida yelped.

"You should not have waited so long to open the doorway," the man answered. "We sent the invitations well in advance."

"But the keys only started glowing yesterday," Rachel said.

The man looked startled. "Oh, it must take longer for magic to reach your land than we thought. Well, don't worry. Allowances will be made."

"OK, look," Kaida said. "We have to go work on our presents. Any other stuff about how we're supposed to act, you can tell us in the morning. So, um, bye." She reached out and snatched her Realm key from the wall, and the doorway vanished. Then she turned around with a panicked look on her face. "Presents? How are we going to come up with presents by tomorrow?"

CHAPTER TWO
Party Day

Shaylee studied the wrapped present lying on the desk before her and wondered if it needed more flowers. Finally, she glued a small silk butterfly on instead and decided it looked as good as it was going to. She scooped it up and slipped it into her dance bag.

Hurrying toward the clubhouse in the middle of the park, she caught sight of Rissa. Her present was wrapped in brightly colored comic strips with a fluffy scarf tied around it.

"Your gift wrap really looks wild," Shaylee said.

"You know that's how I like it," Rissa responded with a grin.

The girls hurried into the clubhouse where the others had already gathered. "How come I always seem to be last?" Shaylee asked.

"Because Aly's moving faster these days," Rachel said with a laugh.

"Hey," Aly said, "I wasn't *always* last."

"Not always," Kaida said. "There was that time Marisol turned her ankle. She was definitely slower than you then."

"For a couple days, as I remember," Marisol said, looking up from her package where she was tying on some bells and ribbons threaded with beads.

"Are we ready to go?" Kaida asked. Her present was the largest, but almost flat. It was wrapped in plain brown paper that Kaida had stamped all over with different dragon stamps and then tied with twine. It was cool looking, in a totally Kaida way.

"What's your gift?" Shaylee asked.

"That cross-stitch dragon picture I've been working on," Kaida said. "I worked like crazy half the night getting it done and framed."

"Oh, that picture is gorgeous!" Marisol exclaimed, as they walked to the wall to place their Realm keys. "My painted seashell is going to look totally lame next to that."

Shaylee's stomach clenched as each of her friends placed their keys on the wall. She hoped her gift was a hit, but mostly she hoped this visit wouldn't be as scary as the last one. With a trembling hand, she placed her key last and then held her breath as they waited for the window to the Realm to appear.

The smooth wall seemed to fade away, and they saw a brightly lit morning on a bustling cobblestone street. Almost immediately they heard an excited squeal, and a friendly green face popped into view.

"Princesses!" said the green-haired girl, who was one of the Meadow Folk who lived in the Village of the Realm.

"Eidermoss!" Shaylee cried. She was delighted to see the friendly face instead of the grouchy man she was expecting.

Eidermoss tried to hug Shaylee right through the narrow gap but got stuck in the hole. She wiggled, and the gap widened. Then the other girls pulled the opening wider so they could step through.

"I'm so glad you came," Eidermoss gushed excitedly. "Thorny said you were coming, but he talks so much and so long that sometimes I fall asleep, and I'm not always sure exactly what he said."

"Thorny?" Rissa asked.

Eidermoss giggled. "That's his nickname. Not that we say it *to* him. But he is prickly, don't you think?"

"Not to mention bossy," Kaida added. "Where is he?"

"Oh, someone put the wrong flowers in entirely the wrong spot," Eidermoss said, imitating the grumpy man's high-pitched rant. Then she giggled again. "I agreed to meet you and make sure you were *appropriate*."

"And are we?" Shaylee asked nervously.

"Oh, you're wonderful," Eidermoss said. "But you might want to change your clothes. Everyone will be wearing dance dresses. Well, everyone except the menfolk that is."

"OK," Rachel said. "We made our clothes change the last time we were here. We just hold hands and kind of imagine—right?"

The girls nodded and joined hands. Then Shaylee said, "Maybe you could hold hands with us too, Eidermoss, to help. You could think about what might be nice for us to wear."

Eidermoss squealed with joy and rushed over to join hands with the others. Then they closed their eyes. Shaylee pictured something like a dance costume, long and swirling. She could feel the bodice of the dress smooth against her skin like satin and the skirt flow in layers down her legs. She pictured dancing slippers and felt them gently hug her feet. Then her eyes popped open, and she looked around.

Her own dress was her favorite shades of pink and green. Each of the other girls had similar flowing dresses, except for Kaida. Her bodice was smoothly fitted leather, and she wore knee-length pants in buttery-colored thin leather as well; long strips of pale fabric hung from her leather waistband to make a kind of skirt.

"Hey," Rissa said as she looked over Kaida's outfit. "You're really rockin' the warrior-princess look today."

Kaida shrugged. "I don't really do dainty."

Rissa looked at her own wildly colored dress and said, "I wish I'd seen yours before I thought up mine."

Shaylee patted her friend's arm. "I think your dress looks great. It's like a paint store exploded."

Rissa grinned. "That does make me feel better."

"We should go," Eidermoss said, reaching out to tug on Shaylee's arm. "I'll show you where the gifts belong, and then we can meet everyone. When they heard you were coming, Folk from all over began pouring into town to see their princesses." She dropped her voice as if ready to tell a big secret. "I even met three of the Guardians!"

Picking up her pace to walk beside Eidermoss, Rachel asked, "Really? Did you hear their names?"

"Oh, I am sure I did," Eidermoss said, "but I've heard so many names, I don't remember what they were."

The group passed through several narrow streets paved with smooth flat stones. The buildings on either side crowded close to the street. Though similar in design, clearly the owners of the homes had worked to put their own stamp on each. One house had wreaths of vine and flowers surrounding each round window. Another house had animals carved into the posts that supported the walls.

Finally, the narrow street opened onto a huge open meadow where a few of the Folk stood in groups with one person in each group pointing at spots around the area and giving orders. Shaylee wondered if they had come too early, as it seemed so few people had arrived.

"Should we have waited?" she asked Eidermoss. "Hardly anyone is here."

Eidermoss giggled. "People will be coming and going until the formal procession. There's so much to prepare." Then she pointed toward a structure across the meadow and said, "Besides, the important things are already here."

Shaylee looked in the direction Eidermoss gestured. Near one end of the field a tall pyramid, built from wood, held hundreds of gifts. The wooden pyramid looked a bit like four sports bleachers with their back sides facing. On every "seat" lay large and small packages. Some were neatly square and wrapped in bits of fabric and lace. Some were oddly shaped and covered with what looked like green leaves tied with string. A couple even wiggled a bit as the girls walked closer to add their gifts and marvel at the amazing wrappings.

"Look at this one," Rissa said, tugging Shaylee's hand. The package looked exactly like a massive egg wrapped in flowering vine. "What do you think hatches from this?"

Eidermoss peered at it and shrugged. "I probably wouldn't pick it. It looks like it might contain something that would be hard to feed."

"You could fit a small pony in there," Kaida said.

The young green girl looked at her seriously. "Ponies hardly ever lay eggs."

Shaylee twisted her hands nervously. She hoped whoever got her gift didn't think it was stupid. She jumped when she heard someone call her name. Shaylee turned and was surprised to see a laughing girl about her own age running toward her, honey-blond hair bouncing as she ran. "I'm so glad you came," the girl gushed.

Shaylee blinked. "Do I know you?"

The girl laughed again, and then she gave a pretend pout. "You didn't see me long enough in this form to remember me. But in one of my other forms, you saved my life from the plant that was trying to strangle me."

"Honeyglow!" Shaylee squealed and hugged her friend who she'd known in her Guardian bear form.

Honeyglow turned then to bow slightly to Rachel. "Fleet sends his greetings, Princess of the Guarded Forest," she said. "He could not come to the party because it is his turn to guard the Wellspring."

"Oh." Rachel's face reflected every bit of her disappointment. "Tell him I'm sorry that he couldn't come."

Honeyglow bowed again and then linked arms with Shaylee. "It's almost time for the gifting to begin. This is my first Feast Cycle Celebration."

"Mine too," Shaylee said. "I'm scared to death that I'll do the wrong thing."

Honeyglow laughed. "You are the princess of these people. Anything you do today will become all the fashion tomorrow."

More and more people filtered into the open meadow. Shaylee spotted several of the Mud Shapers Folk who had given each of the princesses a beautiful and magical bead containing an image that related to each girl's special power. Then she caught sight of the prissy etiquette teacher who was supposed to instruct them on how to behave at the Celebration; he was looking their way and frowning slightly at the sight of Kaida's outfit. Shaylee giggled and waved at him. He carefully imitated her finger wiggling wave and nodded.

Eidermoss stepped up beside Shaylee and rested her hand on Shaylee's arm, making her jump. "It's time," Eidermoss whispered.

"Time for what?" Shaylee whispered back, but before her friend could answer, they heard the bright tinkle of bells as if hundreds of wind chimes rang at once. Every head turned toward the sound, and Shaylee saw a small procession of adults in colorful clothes walking into the clearing carrying golden poles, each with several crosspieces. From the crosspieces, ribbons strung with bells moving gently as they walked.

The procession stopped near the gifts, and each pole was fitted into a slot around the perimeter of the gift pyramid. Then a tall woman with snow white hair and very pale green skin turned to face the crowd. "Welcome to the Celebration to honor the return of the Princesses of the Realm!"

The crowd burst into applause and cheering. Shaylee felt her face flush as Eidermoss gently pushed her toward the front. She was met by her friends, who were also being shoved forward.

"Princesses," the woman said, "we, the Members of the Meadow Folk living in the Realm of Wellspring, are grateful for the return of Wellspring, our source of goodness and life. Without your courage and cleverness, our land would have died. All that we have is yours."

Again the crowd burst into cheers and applause, and Shaylee could see her friends looked as embarrassed as she felt.

The woman smiled at the girls gently, and when the cheers quieted, she said, "I am Willowdawn, leader of the Meadow Dancers. We welcome you to the dance, our princesses. And from all over the Realm, our people bring gifts. This is for you, Princess of the Folk." She held out a bundle wrapped in what looked like silk scarves to Shaylee.

Shaylee took it with trembling hands and gently

unfolded the beautiful silks. Inside lay a tiny dancer carved from crystal. "Oh, she's beautiful!" Shaylee gasped.

"Hold out your hand, Princess," the woman said. Then she stood the crystal dancer in the palm of Shaylee's hand, and the tiny figure began to dance while faint strains of music filled the air.

"Oh my," Shaylee said as tears filled her eyes. "This is the most beautiful thing I've ever seen."

Willowdawn smiled. "We are grateful that you like our dancer. May I benefit from your gift?"

Shaylee's mouth opened as her face flushed again. The old pair of ballet slippers she had trimmed with ribbons and silk flowers was horrible compared to the magical crystal dancer. Surely, they would laugh at her gift!

Eidermoss leaned close to Shaylee and whispered, "You have to say, 'yes.'"

"Yes," Shaylee squeaked.

Quickly someone carried Shaylee's gift to Willowdawn. The regal-looking woman smiled appreciatively at the silk flowers and butterfly on the wrappings, and then she opened the gift and exclaimed, "Oh, dancing shoes! And they're lovely."

Willowdawn slipped the ballet shoes on her feet, and they instantly adjusted to fit perfectly. Then the silk ribbons Shaylee had added magically wrapped themselves around the Meadow Dancer's legs in an intricate pattern that reached nearly to the hem of the woman's silky golden dress. Silk roses bloomed on the toes of the shoes. The older woman tentatively danced a few steps to the cheers of the audience. "They are so beautiful, Princess. Thank you."

Shaylee just gaped. How had her old slippers changed into something so beautiful?

Then Honeyglow hurried to the front and turned to the audience. "The Guardians offer their gratitude to the princesses for the return of our magic, setting us free from the form that held us. We have a gift for the Princess of the Guarded Forest."

Rachel stepped forward, and Honeyglow held out a beautifully carved wooden box. Rachel opened it and lifted out a wooden flute that seemed to be made from many kinds of wood fashioned together. She put the flute to her lips, and music so lovely poured out that soon everyone in the meadow was dancing and laughing.

Finally, Rachel pulled the flute from her lips. "That's the most wonderful thing I've ever received!"

Honeyglow clapped her hands in delight. "I'm so glad. Fleet made it himself. Now, may I benefit from your gift?"

Rachel agreed shyly, and someone brought Rachel's gift, which was wrapped in bright white paper stamped with animal tracks and tied with a big plaid bow. Honeyglow opened it and grinned as she took out the tiny fluffy bear that Rachel had made from soft brown yarn wound into thick pompoms and strung on wire so that he could be put in different positions. Shiny black-button eyes seemed to sparkle with mischief. "He's so cute," Honeyglow said, gently petting the tiny bear in the palm of her hand. Suddenly, the miniature bear changed from a lifeless doll into a moving and breathing animal. He looked around and growled a tiny growl, shaking out his fur as if he had just awakened from a long winter's nap.

"I love him!" said Honeyglow.

Then Spindlethorne of the Mud Shapers Folk stepped forward. He was the leader of the Beadmakers; the girls had met him during their quest to save Wellspring. His head was still decorated with the same careful leopard-spot design they'd seen before, painted on with mud.

He turned to look at Kaida. "Princess of the Bright Sky," he said, "I stand before you on behalf of the Warrior People of the Bright Sky, as they cannot be here." He paused a moment, and everyone in the meadow bowed their heads in a moment in silence. Shaylee and her friends exchanged questioning looks. Then Spindlethorne continued, "Thank you for bringing the magic back to our world, Princesses. We humbly gift you with this." He held out a small, flat ceramic box.

Kaida opened it and smiled as she lifted out a beautiful beaded bracelet done in shades of gold and brown with silvery blue beads for accent. She slipped the bracelet on her arm.

"The golden beads represent your gift of fire and will help strengthen your control of the gift," Spindlethorne said. "The blue represents the sky, and the brown represents the soil—you have gifts with these elements as well that you have yet to unlock. When you do, the magic in this bracelet will help you to do what you need to do."

"Thank you," Kaida said. "It's gorgeous." Then she

flashed a smile at her friend Marisol. "I might turn into a jewelry girl yet."

At that, the crowd laughed and clapped their agreement. Then Spindlethorne asked, "May I benefit from your gift?"

Kaida agreed, her eyes still on the mysterious and beautiful bracelet.

"I'll get it for you," Rachel said. She quickly carried over the large flat package Kaida had brought.

Shaylee leaned forward, interested to see Spindlethorne's reaction to Kaida's gift. Then suddenly it hit her that Kaida's gift was a cross-stitched dragon—and Rachel had just touched it! Rachel's power was tied to the animals. What if that power brought the dragon to life too?

CHAPTER THREE
The Emerald Dragon

In the sunny meadow, the crowd had gradually pressed forward to see each princess's gift. The slow push of the crowd had edged Shaylee away from her friends. As she turned in a tight circle, she didn't see a single face she knew close by. She struggled now to reach the front and say something about Kaida's gift, but she found it difficult to weave through the excited crowd.

Finally, instead of pressing against the people around her, she bent low and slipped through small spaces between people and was able to make slow progress forward.

Maybe it would be OK, she hoped. Maybe the dragon would stay tiny like the little bear Rachel had made. She stopped and took a deep breath. She was probably just being silly.

She stretched up on her toes and searched the faces around her for any she knew. That's when she caught sight of a thatch of cotton-candy pink hair. She shouted for her friend, but there was so much noise from the crowd that Rissa never turned to look. So Shaylee bent low again and wiggled through the press of bodies until she was standing beside Rissa.

Shaylee leaned close to her friend's ear. "Do you think it'll be OK?"

"Why wouldn't it be?" Rissa asked.

"It's a picture of a dragon, remember? And Rachel just touched it."

"But it's only about six inches long," Rissa said. "Spindlethorne can use it to light candles."

Shaylee's eyes went wide. She hadn't thought at all about it breathing fire! It wouldn't have to be very big to make a very big problem. She crossed her fingers and turned her attention back to the group at the gift pyramid.

They watched Spindlethorne unwrap the brown paper from around the framed picture. Shaylee thought Kaida had done a gorgeous job. The dragon sparkled in metallic thread against the rich dark blue of the cross-stitch cloth. Then, the dragon seemed to move within the picture, sweeping its long emerald green wings faster and faster as it hovered in the center of the frame and peered out at the people around it.

"It is magnificent!" Spindlethorne said, smiling widely. He held up the picture so the crowd could see, and Shaylee heard the cheer of approval at the beautiful dragon.

Shaylee let out a pent-up breath in relief. Surely it

was perfectly safe to have a moving picture. It would be wonderful if the ballerinas in the pictures on the walls of her room would start dancing like that.

The tiny dragon continued to beat its wings faster and faster. Finally, it broke free from the canvas and flew in sweeping circles around Spindlethorne and Kaida. Kaida turned in the circle to follow the flight of the small metallic green dragon, her face shining with delight. But Shaylee could already see the little dragon was growing with each circle around the Beadmaker and her friend.

At first it was only the size of Shaylee's two outstretched hands. Then it was as big as a small cat. Then it grew to the size of a small dog, and its wingspan stretched wider than Shaylee could reach with both arms. The crowd gasped and murmured anxiously.

Shaylee wondered again about the possibility that the dragon might breathe fire. She looked around at the thatched roofs on the homes and at the delicate pile of gifts. If the dragon did breathe fire, the party would definitely be over, and the people could lose their homes. Again Shaylee struggled to push through the crowd with Rissa at her side.

The dragon continued to circle and grow. Its flapping wings created an increasingly stronger wind. The bells on the poles jangled frantically. Packages tumbled from the gift pyramid, and the crowd backed away farther and farther. Still, there was no sign of fire.

"Perhaps," Spindlethorne shouted over the swoosh of

the dragon's wings, "you could tell me how to make it stop?"

Kaida's delighted face now filled with alarm. "I don't know. It didn't do this at my house. It was just a picture."

The dragon flapped its massive wings to circle half the pasture. It had grown too big to keep the same tight formation over Kaida and Spindlethorne. The beating of its wings nearly drowned out the murmurs and cries of the crowd as it flew around the whole meadow. It had reached the size of a pony with immense wings. The Folk of the Realm now simply turned and ran for the narrow streets of the village where this new huge dragon couldn't possibly fit.

"Where did Rachel go?" Shaylee asked as the crowd around her broke apart to run. "She needs to do something to control this wild animal!"

"Maybe I could try a spell," Rissa suggested. "Something to make it shrink."

Rachel stumbled up beside her friends. The wind from the dragon's wings made it hard to walk. She reached her hands toward the sky and called, "Come here! Come and land!"

The dragon continued to circle, and Rachel turned to Kaida with a helpless shrug. "I thought it might listen to me since the animals in the forest do."

"It is not of the Guarded Forest," Honeyglow said, stepping close to the girls and watching the dragon's flight. "It can choose to listen to you, but it is not bound by your commands."

"But she's the one who brought it to life with her power, isn't she?" Shaylee asked. "She touched the picture. It should listen to her."

"In the Realm, things aren't always that simple," Honeyglow said.

Rachel frowned. "Sorry, Kaida."

"Don't be. This is probably the coolest thing I've ever made. Scary, but cool."

"This dragon is a creature of the air," Honeyglow said. She turned to Kaida. "You created it. It may obey you."

Kaida nodded. The fierce wind from the dragon's wings had begun to blow the thatch from the nearest buildings, and the girls knew they needed to do something before their gift destroyed the village. Kaida scrambled to the top of the wooden gift pyramid, gently nudging gifts aside as she climbed. She held out her arms and yelled, "Come to me, dragon!"

The dragon veered from its circular course immediately. It flew directly at Kaida with its huge jaws open. Abruptly it stopped and hung in the air in front of Kaida. Massive wings beat the air to hold it in a hover. The wind blew the rest of the gifts from the pyramid. The girl and the dragon stared at one another for a moment, and then the dragon rushed toward her.

Shaylee screamed as the dragon's sharp beak barely missed her friend. Then it pivoted in the air, and Kaida was caught in the angle between the creature's neck and wing. She tumbled onto its back and clung desperately.

The dragon roared, and the sound made the ground under Shaylee's feet shake. Once again, it began to circle the meadow, but this time, each circle took it higher into the sky.

Aly ran to an arbor that ran along a stone wall. Grapevines grew thick on the arbor, making a shady spot underneath where benches offered a quiet place to sit. Earlier, the arbor had been the resting spot for the older visitors, but now it was empty as every one of the Folk had fled the meadow. Aly thrust her hands into the vines and closed her eyes.

Immediately, the vines whipped into the air, forming snares to snatch at the dragon's legs and tail as it circled. The dragon dodged them easily until a single vine snared the creature's tail. It jerked the dragon to a sudden stop, and Shaylee screamed as Kaida nearly tumbled from the dragon's back. The dragon twisted his long neck and snapped through the vine, even as new vines grabbed for the creature's snout.

The dragon roared. Then it flew a final circle around the grassy meadow with their friend clinging to its back before turning away from the village and flying at incredible speed toward the distant mountains.

"Kaida!" Shaylee screamed as she ran across the meadow, following the path of the dragon as far as she could. But the dragon, with her friend on its back, quickly vanished from sight.

Honeyglow and her other friends ran up beside her.

"Don't worry," Rissa said. "We'll get her back."

Rachel turned to the Guardian. "Do you know what's off in that direction?"

"A very dense woodland," Honeyglow said. "It connects to the Guarded Forest, but that area isn't really part of our domain. The paths through it are wide and straight. Then after that, you'll reach the rocky shore and the Living Waters Sea, where your people live, Marisol. But if you cross that sea, you'd reach the Mountains of the Frozen Sky. I feel sure that is where the dragon would go."

"Why?" Marisol asked.

Honeyglow turned and looked at the girls solemnly. "That is where the Warrior People of the Bright Sky lived before they left the Realm. The dragon is still Kaida's creation and fueled by her magic. It is logical that it would be drawn to the home of her people."

Rachel crossed her arms over her chest and said, "So how do we get there?"

"You can walk through the woodland, though it will take a long time," the Guardian said. "And with a boat, you can cross the sea, especially with the help of Marisol's people. And you will likely find other help once you get to the mountains, though few of the Folk can withstand the bitter cold there."

Rissa ran a hand through her pink hair, making it stand up in places. "That sounds like a trip that could take a couple years. We need to get to Kaida now. She is definitely not dressed for bitter cold."

"There must be a way to save our friend," Aly said quietly, and all the girls nodded.

At that moment, Spindlethorne finally caught up to the girls. He had fled with the other Meadow Folk, but now he returned, puffing slightly from crossing the field quickly. "You must not go! The sea is filled with monsters, and the mountains are haunted."

Honeyglow snorted at that, and Spindlethorne turned to her sharply. "The princesses must not risk their lives on such a dangerous quest."

"Dangerous like restoring Wellspring?" Rachel asked.

"Dangerous like fighting blood-drinking plants and giant spiders?" Rissa said.

"And almost drowning in the river?" Shaylee added.

"Dangerous like flying through the air over the trees?" Marisol asked.

Then the girls turned to one another and grinned. "That's a great idea. Rissa can do another spell so we can fly from here to the mountains," Rachel said. "That's how we can save Kaida!"

"Only no dumping us in the mud," Shaylee said, her voice a bit shaky. "It took me a week to feel really clean after that."

"I think I can help with that," Aly said. "If we head out to the woodland, I could ask the plants to weave us a boat of sorts. Then Rissa could enchant the boat to fly. And we could make some kind of rudder to steer with. At the very least, if we fall out of the sky, we'll have something between us and the mud."

The girls nodded, exchanging smiles. It sounded like a perfect plan.

"No, no, no," Spindlethorne said. "I really must insist that you not go off on such a dangerous and impulsive journey. We should gather the Folk and hear from the different elders. I'm sure they will have excellent ideas."

"And while they're chatting," Rissa said, "Kaida could be dragon food."

"I do not think the dragon will intentionally hurt Kaida," Honeyglow said. "She did create him." The girls looked relieved at that, until the Guardian added, "But the mountains have their own dangers, and they are very cold."

"Then it's decided," Rissa said, "we go—right?"

She turned to the others, and they all nodded, though Shaylee felt a flutter of fear in her stomach. She did not like the idea of flying again, and she definitely wasn't eager to meet the dangers of the mountains. What had happened to the nice fun party?

CHAPTER FOUR
The Journey Begins

The girls followed Honeyglow back through the streets toward the nearest access to the woodland. None of them spoke much. Worry about Kaida gnawed at Shaylee's stomach, making her feel shaky. She felt desperate to get started so they could save their friend, and at that same time, she was nearly terrified by the idea of what they might encounter.

As they walked through the streets, people peered nervously from the doorways. A few stepped out to press wrapped bundles of food or warm clothes into the girls' hands. One young girl handed Shaylee a flask of water that hung from an elaborately carved belt. With each gift, the giver would glance nervously at the sky above as if expecting the dragon to come swooping down upon them.

Rissa stepped close to Shaylee and whispered, "Wow, we really know how to make an impression with presents."

Shaylee nodded, and then smiled a little. "At least mine

was just a pair of shoes," she said. "What were you giving?"

"A poem," Rissa said. "I wrote it on a piece of canvas in calligraphy."

Shaylee looked at her. "Since your poems seem to be spells here, you might want to think about getting that one back."

"I'm not sure. It's about my cat, and I even stenciled a row of cats across the bottom. Seems a lot more harmless than a dragon."

"Let's hope," Shaylee said. As she was wondering if anything bad would happen if a row of stenciled cats jumped off a piece of paper, the street they were walking on began to widen. Finally, they came to a wall with a tall gate.

"This gate leads to the woodland," Honeyglow said to the girls. Then she shouted out to the gatekeepers, "Open for the Guardian of the Forest and the Princesses of the Realm!"

Shaylee looked up at narrow windows in the thick walls on either side of the gate. Pale green faces peered from the windows; they nodded and disappeared. The large heavy doors of the gate began to open slowly. She saw a clearing beyond, and then a wide path into the woods.

As the girls hurried through the gate, Shaylee glanced back. A small group of the Folk stood in the street looking after them. She smiled and waved, and they waved back solemnly. Then the doors swung shut behind them.

Honeyglow didn't slow down until they had walked for several minutes along the wide woodland path. Then she turned to face Aly. "Is this far enough? Can you make your boat here?"

Aly stepped from the path into the thick forest and seemed to be looking for something on the forest floor. She stopped near a long, straight piece of fallen branch. She walked around it and must have made some decision because she finally stopped near one end.

Aly closed her eyes. The woodland seemed almost to lean in closer to the quiet girl. Then, a bit of ivy slipped down from the tree closest to her and touched her gently on the cheek. Aly's eyes stayed closed, and the ivy trailed on down to the ground.

More ivy slipped from other trees and crept over to join the first. The vines began sliding along the fallen branch. Some of it slipped under the log and then out the other side. More ivy joined in, weaving together with the previous strands.

At first, it appeared to be making a long, narrow basket with the branch acting as a kind of thick backbone at the curved bottom. Then more strands crossed the center, making slings where a person could sit. After that, the walls grew higher until the whole structure reached nearly to Aly's shoulder.

Then, to Shaylee's shock, a sapling near Aly bent far over, thrusting a branch into the rear of the small ship while more vines lashed it loosely in place. The sapling branch bent down from the back of the ship, and the shape of the branch changed from rounded to flat like a rudder. Then it simply pinched off from the rest of the small tree. The little tree stood back up with a healed scar where the branch had once been.

Finally, the little boat was done. Aly opened her eyes and turned to smile at her friends. "Now we have a boat to fly in."

Marisol grinned at Rissa. "You're up. If you drop us in the mud this time, at least we can keep our clothes clean."

"Are you going to come with us?" Shaylee asked Honeyglow.

Honeyglow wrinkled her nose slightly. "I don't think I'd enjoy flying. I prefer to keep my paws firmly on the ground."

"How will we know which way to go?" Aly asked.

"Head toward the setting sun, and you'll reach the mountains," Honeyglow said, pointing the way. "You might even want to put that in your spell."

"OK, we should get in first, I think," Rissa said.

The girls each gave Honeyglow a quick hug and then scrambled into the boat.

"Wait," Marisol said. "Shouldn't we have a mast and sail? I mean if this is a boat, doesn't it need a sail?"

"The villagers gave us some blankets," Aly said. "We could use one for a sail."

"Let me help with the mast," Honeyglow said. The golden-haired girl stepped a few paces away from the boat until she stood in the middle of the path. She closed her eyes and seemed to glow. Then her light hair began to grow so fast it flowed over her shoulders like a river. It grew until the girl was enrobed in golden hair that hid her shape. The hooded cape of golden hair transformed into the outline of a bear, standing on her back legs. As the glow faded, their friend appeared as the golden bear they had met during their quest to save Wellspring.

Honeyglow dropped down onto all four legs and trotted off into the woods. She returned in a few minutes with a tall, straight trunk of a sapling clenched in her teeth. She carried it over to the side of the boat, and the princesses worked together to haul it into place as a center mast. Then Aly had the vines reform to hold the new mast in place.

As the girls held up a beautiful sea green blanket that one of the Folk had handed them as they passed through the town, more vines slipped down from the trees and fashioned crosspieces for the mast to hold the blanket in place as a sail.

"Now, we're ready," Marisol said as she admired the beautiful blanket.

"OK, let me give this a try," Rissa said. She took a deep breath and said,

Take our boat into the sky,
Toward the setting sun we fly,
Just over the green woodland,
Right over the silver sea,
Take us to the mountains high,
Mountains of the Frozen Sky.

The vine ship quivered and then began slowly to lift as if bobbing on a rising river. Shaylee leaned over the side of the boat slightly and waved hard. "Goodbye, Honeyglow!"

Rachel and Rissa leaned over to join her and wave to the golden bear. Since Aly was already near Shaylee, the sudden change in position caused the boat to tilt sharply.

"No!" Marisol shrieked. "We're unbalanced."

The sudden tilt caused Shaylee to flip over the side of the flying ship. Fortunately, she had held onto the vine railing with one hand, and that was all that saved her from falling. Rachel and Rissa quickly grabbed hold of her hands, and both reached down to grasp the leather belt Shaylee had fastened around her waist. As they tried to haul her back onboard, their combined weight still caused the boat to tilt even more sharply

Thinking quickly, Aly flung herself toward the other side of the boat near Marisol to help balance the load and lessen the steep tilt. Shaylee shrieked as she dangled from the boat and watched the ground grow farther and farther away.

When she'd fallen overboard on the river during their last visit to the Realm, Shaylee had thought that was the worst thing that could happen to her. Now as she looked at the massive drop looming beneath her, she knew this fall would be deadly.

Rachel and Rissa held on to their friend, but with the boat so badly canted over, they couldn't pull her in.

"I think I have an idea," Rachel said to Rissa. "Can you hold her?"

"Don't drop me!" Shaylee yelled.

"I won't," Rissa said. "I've got you."

Rachel released her grip and edged to the center of the badly unbalanced ship. She pulled the wooden flute that

Fleet had made for her from a pocket in her dress and brought it to her lips. She closed her eyes and played. The music seemed full of chirps and trills. Then, they heard the sound of birds—hundreds of birds—calling and flapping as they flew up to the airborne boat. Eagles and hawks caught hold of the vines that made the railing of the boat on either side of Shaylee. They beat their wings fiercely to lift the low side.

Meanwhile hundreds of songbirds landed on the high side of the boat, each adding its tiny weight to help balance the boat. The larger eagles and hawks fought to raise the low side of the boat, and slowly, the boat began to level out.

Rissa hauled backward as hard as she could, dragging Shaylee into the boat. Both girls landed in a pile in the center of the boat. Marisol and Aly shifted to the center as well. The birds released the sides and flapped serenely away.

Rachel opened her eyes and grinned. "That was so cool."

"Not from where I was hanging," Shaylee said.

"Are you OK?" Aly asked, giving the younger girl a hug.

"I'm fine," Shaylee said. "Just a little freaked out."

Rissa slowly stood and looked around. "Hey, we're flying!"

Carefully the girls moved to places where they could see the land below them. The ship had stopped rising and now sailed along through the sky as if riding a stiff breeze. The tops of the trees below them looked like rounded green hills.

"Too bad Kaida didn't see this spell," Rissa said. "Since we can sit back and relax for a while, maybe we could have some lunch?"

The girls opened packages of food they had been given by the village Folk. They found buttery-tasting cheeses in shades of gold and thick slices of fresh bread. Another package held strips that tasted a little like beef jerky. Still another held tiny cubes of cake that were sweet and nutty at the same time. They also had a small sack filled with pieces of bright blue fruit that were crunchy and tart.

"We shouldn't eat everything," Aly warned. "We don't know how long this trip is going to take." They settled on each having a small bit of everything, which left plenty for another couple of small meals.

"I wish we could get this fruit back in Connecticut," Rissa said. "I think it's my new favorite. It's like a crunchy berry."

"It would be good on oatmeal," Shaylee said as she nibbled on one.

Rissa wrinkled her nose. "Ewww. You eat oatmeal?"

"I like it."

"It looks like something someone already ate once," Rissa said.

"Oh, that's disgusting," Shaylee said.

"Right. Oatmeal is disgusting."

"Let's not fight," Rachel said as she gave Rissa a playful shove. "I kind of like oatmeal, too, though I'm not sure I'll be able to ever look at it the same now. Thanks, pal."

"I just call them like I see them."

Shaylee turned her back on Rissa's gross talk and noticed Marisol perched near the very front point of the boat, staring ahead with intense concentration. Shaylee carefully crept closer to the older girl. "What are you looking at?" she asked.

"The water," Marisol said softly, and her voice sounded dreamy. "There's so much water."

Shaylee recognized the tone of Marisol's voice. She'd gotten all dreamy like that just before the River Dragon dumped them into the water during their last visit. Carefully Shaylee peeked over the edge. She didn't see any monstrous creatures, but she did see water.

Ahead, the woodland ended with a rocky shore that fell away to reveal a huge expanse of water, stretching as far ahead as Shaylee could see. Light danced upon the face of the waves, turning the water to a silvery hue.

"Water ahead," she called back to her friends.

"Can we go down closer?" Marisol asked, her voice eager.

"I don't know if that's a good idea," Rachel said. "The last time you got around water, you went a little crazy."

"I'll be good," Marisol insisted. "I just want to see."

"I can use the rudder, I think, to steer closer," Aly said. "If everyone thinks that is something we should do, that is. We wouldn't have to go too low."

The girls looked at each other, and then nearly everyone nodded eagerly at Aly. Shaylee only managed a nervous shrug. Sure, she wanted to see the beautiful water more closely, but who knew what might live just below the surface?

CHAPTER FIVE
The Crystal Dolphins

With a nod, Aly took hold of the rudder and maneuvered the boat down until it skimmed just over the surface of the water. Each of the girls chose a different spot at the side of the boat so that the load would stay even. They'd not forgotten how easy it was to tip the magical craft, and no one wanted an unexpected bath—with the possible exception of Marisol. She stayed at the front of the boat, her eyes still dreamy.

Shaylee reached out a hand to feel the spray from the waves. She took a deep breath and smelled the sharp scent of ocean. Even though she couldn't swim, she had to admit it was incredibly beautiful.

Suddenly, something leaped out of the water close to her side of the boat. Shaylee shrieked as the creature seemed to sail through the air in a smooth easy arc before plunging back into the water. She honestly couldn't believe her eyes. She'd seen a dolphin, but it wasn't like any living dolphin she'd ever seen. The animal was completely transparent as if it were made of glass or crystal.

Then another dolphin burst from the water a bit farther away. Light shining through the creature's crystal fins broke up and cast rainbows of color through the sky before the dolphin vanished back into the water.

Shaylee turned. "Do you see them?"

"Crystal dolphins," Rachel said. "I can't believe it!"

"They want to fly," Marisol called out. "They're trying to fly like us."

More and more of the beautiful dolphins sailed out of the water in perfect arcs and then vanished again beneath the waves. The girls were flying through a whole pod of the wonderful dolphins.

"They're laughing," Marisol said. "They're so happy to see us."

"I wish I could hear them," Rachel said. "I can't believe how beautiful they are."

They continued to fly along with the dolphin pod, and soon the boat seemed to be completely surrounded with rainbows and the joyful crystal creatures. Shaylee thought it looked like a kind of dance as dolphins leapt from the water in unison, casting off drops of water like diamonds in the sunlight.

All the girls were laughing with joy at the dolphins around them. Then suddenly, Shaylee tumbled into the center of the boat as it slammed to a sudden stop, hitting the surface of the water hard.

"What was that?" Rissa yelled.

"Something caught hold of the trailing vines," Aly said.

The boat lurched again as whatever held them down pulled still harder. "We're taking on water," Rissa said. "Something's pulling us down!"

The boat sank lower and lower in the water until the sea poured over every side. Shaylee screamed, clutching the side of the boat.

"Shaylee, come here!" Marisol shouted. "I can keep you above water."

Shaylee tried to slosh through the water in the small boat to reach her friend, but it was sinking fast. The water pouring over the sides battered her, knocking her over again and again. "Help!" she yelled and then coughed as water sloshed into her mouth.

The boat had sunk completely, and Shaylee was trying to remember what Marisol had said about swimming. Stay calm. If you stay calm, you float.

She *really* hoped she could float. She fought the urge to flail and gasp as she held her breath tightly and focused on calming down. She began to feel herself rise. She was doing it!

Then a hand grabbed her arm. Shaylee's heart soared. One of her friends had found her. She would be OK now. But whoever held her arm wasn't pulling her upward; the person was dragging her down deeper into the water.

Shaylee fought to get free of the grasping hand. Then she felt something binding her legs together like a clenched fist. She couldn't kick them apart but could only swing them together to try to push away the person who gripped her.

As she tried to push her feet against her attacker, she realized she didn't have feet. She had a fin, a tail fin! Shaylee gasped in shock. She was going to drown. Only, she didn't. The water that rushed into her mouth this time didn't make her cough or choke. It didn't burn. It seemed to pass back out through her neck.

Her neck? Shaylee raised her free hand to feel flaps in her neck that opened and closed to let the water rush out after each breath. Gills—she had gills. She turned terrified eyes toward the person who gripped her arm and saw a smiling face in the dark ocean. Suddenly she could see through the water perfectly.

She looked around and saw each of her friends, each being towed by another mermaid. Her friends were mermaids too. With shock, she noticed that not everyone was a mermaid … some were mermen, or merboys with laughing faces.

Finally, the merpeople stopped pulling them downward. A lovely girl with pale blue-green skin swam up to Shaylee and draped a string of pearls around her neck. "Welcome, Princess of the Folk," the girl said.

Tentatively, Shaylee tried talking under the water. "Thank you." Her voice sounded strange and bubbly. "How did I change? Why do I have a tail?"

"Legs are for land," the mermaid said. "No land here. You need a tail. You'll swim fast now. We can play."

"But how did I change?" Shaylee asked.

"We changed you," the mermaid said, "so you could play.

Come and play. Come and chase." The mermaid laughed and splashed away.

Merpeople splashed and swam in circles around the princesses. Shaylee felt a tug at her hair and saw two young mermaids weaving shells into narrow braids in her blonde hair. Shaylee looked around at her friends.

She saw more of the merchildren giggling and fluffing Rissa's chin-length pink hair. Clearly no one could weave shells into her friend's bob. But both Rachel and Aly already had strings of pearls, shells and coral beads mixed with their long curls. And Marisol looked like a true princess with all the finery the mermaids piled on her.

Shaylee swam toward her friend. "We can't stay," she reminded Marisol. "We have to save Kaida."

Marisol nodded and then spoke to the merpeople, "I am so happy to meet all of you. We do want to swim with you and play, but first we must rescue the sixth princess. Our friend is being held prisoner in the Mountains of the Frozen Sky. We have to save her."

"The Mountains of the Frozen Sky!" The words echoed on the lips of merpeople all around them. Some of the smaller children dashed away in a panic at the very words. "You don't want to go to the mountains!"

"You must stay here," an elderly mermaid said. "You must stay safe, dear Princess."

"We cannot stay safe," Marisol said. "Not while our friend is in danger. We have to save her."

Several of the mermaids grabbed at Marisol's hands.

"Stay and play. Stay safe."

"We cannot," Marisol said. "I love seeing you. I would love to swim and play here, but I cannot lose my friend. She would not leave me behind."

The merpeople nodded at that. "Friends do not leave you."

"Can you tell us where our boat is?" Rachel asked as she swam closer with her sister.

"Boat?" the mermaids said. "Mermaids don't need boats."

"We cannot swim as fast as we could fly in our boat," Rissa said. "We need to get to the mountains quickly."

"Your boat won't fly now," the old mermaid said. "It drifted apart with the water."

"Oh no," Shaylee said.

"Fear not, Princess." The mermaid patted her arm gently. "The dolphins are much faster than a boat. They will take you to your friend."

"The dolphins. The crystal dolphins." The word rang like wind chimes around the girls as each of the merpeople echoed what the old one said.

"Call them, Princess," a mermaid said, giggling at Marisol's elbow. "They will answer the Princess. They will swim very fast. Faster even than me!"

"Call them. Call the dolphins."

Marisol called. For several long minutes, they heard only the giggles and splashes of the merpeople who surrounded them. Then in a powerful whoosh, the dolphins arrived.

Shaylee laughed as a crystal dolphin bumped her gently as if asking to be petted. She ran her hand over the dolphin's smooth skin. The dolphin opened its mouth, showing crystal teeth in a wide grin. "You're beautiful," Shaylee said, and the dolphin nodded as if in agreement.

She looked around at her friends and found each of them petting and playing with one of the beautiful dolphins. The creatures were difficult to see if they moved swiftly, but they seemed to shimmer when they stopped and nuzzled each girl's hand.

"The dolphins say that they'll tow us to the shore of the mountains if we grip their top fins," Marisol called out.

"But will they be fast enough?" Rissa asked.

The elderly mermaid laid a hand on Marisol's arm. "You can command the waters, Princess. Call the current to help, and the dolphins will swim faster than they have ever swum before. They will be the shooting stars of the sea."

"Will we be able to hold on if they go so fast?" Shaylee asked.

"The dolphin will look after you, dear Princess," the mermaid said. "Do not be afraid. They will not let you be harmed. Trust them."

As if in agreement, the dolphin beside Shaylee nuzzled her cheek. "I do trust you," the girl said.

"Wait," a small voice called out.

The girls turned to see a very young merchild swimming up with a bag in her hands made from net. "You should take food. On the shore, you can never find such lovely things to eat." She held out the bag.

"Thank you," Marisol said. "What is it?"

"Fruit from the sea fans," the little mergirl said.

"I wouldn't mind a quick bite before we rocket through the water," Rissa said, peeking at the bag.

Smiling, the girl reached into the bag and pulled out a small purple fruit covered with bumps. "You can eat it all, Princess."

Rissa took a bite and then smiled. "Wow, it doesn't taste sweet at all, but with the sea water mixed in, it's yummy."

Each of the girls took a fruit and gobbled it down; then Marisol tied the bag around her waist. "Thank you all for everything. I'm so glad to meet you. We'll come back to see you, I promise."

"Um, quick question," Rachel interjected. "Once we get to land, how do we turn back into girls? We had to use a spell from Rissa last time Marisol changed."

The old mermaid tisked over that. "Princess Marisol, you need only to call on your magic, child. It is full and flowing now with the return of Wellspring. You can change all your friends and yourself, though I see nothing about walking on land that could be as good as swimming."

"I agree," Marisol said, "But since our friend is held prisoner in the mountains, I do think we'll need legs. Thank you again for your help."

The old mermaid took Marisol's face in her delicate hands and gently kissed the girl's cheek. "May the currents be friendly and the sea always sing in your blood."

"Swim well!" The merpeople waved and shouted as each girl took careful hold of the fin of her new crystal dolphin friend. The dolphins flipped their powerful tails, and they took off in a whoosh.

Some of the younger mermaids swam with them as long as they could keep up, but one by one, they dropped away, and it was just the five girls rushing through the water as they clung to the fins of the dolphins.

Suddenly Shaylee felt a fresh surge of power all around her, and the dolphin seemed to swim even faster. Shaylee knew that it must be the current boost that Marisol had called for. The speed with which she rushed through the water was incredibly exciting and more than a little terrifying. She closed her eyes and concentrated on hanging on while she wondered exactly what they would find at the end of the swim.

CHAPTER SIX
The Ice Guardians

At first, clinging to a dolphin as it raced through the fast current was incredibly exciting, but as time passed, the dolphins' up-and-down swimming style began to make Shaylee feel decidedly sick to her stomach.

It reminded her of how queasy she got as a preschool dancer, before she learned to spot on her turns. At her first recital, she had turned and turned and turned in a row with her classmates, all without spotting. On the last turn, she'd thrown up, and the other dancers had to avoid the "Shaylee Sick Slick" for the rest of the dance. Her friends couldn't believe Shaylee hadn't quit dance after such an embarrassing moment, but she couldn't imagine life without dance.

As she thought of the technique of spotting, Shaylee pulled herself a bit more up on the back of the dolphin so she could fix her eyes on a spot ahead. She hoped that since that worked for dancing, it might work for dolphin riding.

Though her stomach didn't settle completely, she did feel a bit better.

Suddenly, her dolphin leaped completely out of the water with Shaylee clinging to its back. In that dazzling jump, she caught her first glimpse of the land ahead. The rocky shore seemed to have no access point, only sheer cliffs and jagged boulders. How were they going to get ashore once they reached it?

The dolphins never hesitated but continued to surge forward with each thrust of their powerful tails. Then, Shaylee noticed they were slowing down. The dolphins seemed to be swimming as strongly as ever, so she suspected the current Marisol had created to push them so quickly had died away.

Finally, the dolphins' strong tail sweeps grew slower and more leisurely. The water no longer raced past Shaylee, pressing her face. She could see more clearly around her, and she saw that the dolphins had gathered in a group. She did a quick head count and blew relieved bubbles as she saw each of her friends.

"This is as far as the dolphins will go," Marisol told them. "They don't want to be trapped in shallow water."

"How do we get on shore?" Shaylee asked. "All I saw were rocks and cliffs."

"The dolphins say there is a small cove very close, but it's too shallow for them," Marisol answered. "We can swim into it and get ashore from there."

"Sounds like a plan," Rissa said.

"I'm going to miss the dolphins," Rachel added wistfully as she patted her dolphin.

"I think we all will," Aly said.

Shaylee gave her own dolphin a hug, and it bumped her gently in response. Then the dolphins turned as a group and headed away from shore. "Goodbye!" Shaylee called after them. "Thank you!"

"This way," Marisol said. "Shaylee, can you swim OK now?"

Shaylee laughed. "Like a fish!"

The girls swam together through the clear icy water. As they ducked under part of an iceberg, the bottom of which extended several yards into the water, Shaylee knew the water must be bitterly cold, but she felt perfectly comfortable. She knew sea mammals stayed warm by lots of body fat, but she assumed mermaids must use some kind of magic. "Yay for magic," she whispered, and the bubbles from her words tickled her nose.

Gradually the water grew more and more shallow. Shaylee could see the rocky bottom where crabs scuttled and waved their long claws at the girls as they swam overhead. Then they came to a wall of rock.

"This is where we climb out," Marisol called. "Use your tail to push yourself upward so you can reach over the rock edge.

Shaylee did as Marisol said and swept her long tail through the water. Her head burst from the water, and she shot upward with the power of her mermaid tail. When her head passed the top of the rock that had made an underwater wall, she grabbed hold and began pulling herself up.

It definitely wasn't one of the more graceful things she'd ever tried to do. Once out of the water, her long tail was virtually useless for moving her along so she had to use her arms. She moved just inches at a time, and the crawl over the rock was exhausting.

Finally, she lay completely out of the water, gasping from the effort. She ran her fingers over her neck and felt her gills, which were completely closed; she could breathe air again. But she still had a long, scaly fishlike tail.

"Can you change us back, Marisol?" Rachel asked, gasping a bit.

"I can try," Marisol said. "I think it'll be easier if we join hands."

This required a bit more wiggling on the rock so that each girl could reach the other. Shaylee was glad to see no one seemed to do that any more gracefully than she did it. She clung to Rissa's hand on her left and Rachel's on her right.

"OK, let me concentrate a moment," Marisol said, closing her eyes.

Shaylee closed her eyes too and tried picturing her own long, slender legs and small feet in case it would help if they all concentrated. She imagined dancing, moving her feet in quick patterns and kicks. Her eyes flew open. She'd felt that kick. She looked down and saw she had her legs again!

Their gowns had magically shrunk to only tops when they grew tails, but now the skirts flowed back over them in a soggy heap. Instantly, the cold air began freezing the fabric into stiff folds.

"Why are we all wet?" Rissa asked, her teeth beginning to chatter. "You weren't wet when you changed back from being a mermaid last time, Marisol."

"You didn't try to change me until I was so dry I was almost sick," Marisol chattered. "That must have made a difference."

"A bad difference," Rachel said. "We have to get warm now, or we're going to freeze to death right here."

The girls staggered to their feet, hugging themselves as they shivered. "I'll try to make a fire," Rissa said, and then she spoke a simple spell:

Wet to dry,
before we die.
Make a fire,
Our need is dire!

Suddenly a rush of warm wind swept around them, and Shaylee was amazed at the feeling of comfort. The warm wind seemed to suck all the dampness from her clothes and hair. Then it settled between the girls and burst into flames.

"Wow," Shaylee said. "You're getting a lot better at this stuff."

Rissa laughed. "Maybe desperation helps."

"This is great, but it doesn't solve our bigger problem," Marisol said. "We can't stay here on the water's edge. We need to climb the mountains and find Kaida. We need help."

Shaylee looked across the icy plateau where they stood. Wind blew bits of ice and snow into the air, making it hard to see very far. Even with the magical fire and warm clothes, it was too cold to be truly comfortable. She couldn't imagine stepping away from the warmth. Could Kaida even survive in this cold?

At least they knew Kaida could make fire. Wherever she was, surely that would keep her alive until they could get to her.

"Something's coming," Rachel said. "I can feel them."

"Some *thing*?" Shaylee said. "Do you know what kind of thing?"

Rachel shook her head. "I'm not completely sure. But they're getting closer; we should see them soon."

The girls peered into the icy mist, taking nervous steps closer to one another and the fire. Then Marisol pointed. "There, I see something moving. Look!"

They squinted. It looked almost as if part of the white mist was clumping together to make a huge white form; then there was another … and another. Shaylee sucked in her breath. Polar bears. They were polar bears.

The biggest bear lumbered up to Rachel and bowed.

"Thank you," Rachel said, clearly hearing voices they could not. "We'll be grateful for your help." She turned to the others. "They're offering us a ride back to where they live. They can help us. They're Guardians too, like Honeyglow and Fleet."

The smallest of the polar bears was easily as big as the other Guardians they'd met. Each bent low to allow one of the girls to scramble up on its back. This time, Rachel and Aly together had to boost Shaylee onto the back of her bear since there were none that were small enough for her to climb up on even when the bears laid almost flat.

The girls clung to the thick fur and pressed close to the warm bears as they lumbered across the icy rocks. Shaylee was glad she already knew how to ride a bear. She giggled, thinking how strange it sounded to know the best way to ride a bear.

Shaylee was very tired, and the bear's gait swayed gently. Soon the girl fell asleep and didn't waken until Rachel and Aly were pulling her from the bear's back. "We're here," Rachel said.

Shaylee blinked. They were inside a huge cavern. The air was warm and dry. The cavern seemed to be lit by glowing crystals embedded in the icy walls. She looked around and saw no fire. "How is it so warm?"

"The Guardians told me this area is volcanic," Rachel said. "They tap into that with magic to make the chambers warm."

The polar bears gathered in front of the girls and then stood on their back legs. They were incredibly tall, and Shaylee felt a shiver of fear as she looked at the long dagger-like claws of the bears. But then, they seemed almost to melt away, leaving a group of young people with snow white hair and dark eyes.

The group of Guardians immediately broke up and began hurrying around to different tasks. A tall girl with a gentle smile brought bowls of hot soup to each of the princesses. Shaylee tasted the soup tentatively and found it thick and delicious. She sat down on a nearby rock and gulped down the soup, finally feeling truly warm to her very core.

Two other Guardians brought warm clothing for each girl. After they were dressed for the cold climate and their stomachs were full, Marisol said, "Do you know where our friend Kaida is?"

The leader of the Guardians, a broad-shouldered boy with brown skin and dark eyes that made his white hair seem to glow, sighed and said, "We saw the dragon come to the Mountains of the Frozen Sky. There have been no dragons here since the last of the Sky Warriors left."

"Why did they leave?" Shaylee asked.

"To save us all," the leader said, "and to save the people of your world as well. It is a long story—too long for this journey. But the dragon has carried your friend to the upper caverns where the Sky Dragons once lived."

The girl who had brought Shaylee the bowl of soup spoke. "We tried to reach her, but we could not get close enough even to see her. I believe the dragon is trying to protect her. The Sky Dragons bonded deeply with their warriors. We do not want to fight it unless we must."

"But that dragon is just something Kaida made," Rachel said, "in cross-stitch."

"I don't know cross-stitch," the girl said, "but perhaps it explains the dragon's strange colors. Still, if the Princess of the Sky made it, then it is sensible to assume it will act like a Sky Dragon."

"Do you think Kaida is OK?" Marisol asked.

"We have not seen her, and that is troubling. The

dragon will protect her with its own life," the leader said, "but I doubt it can feed her, nor can it heal her if she is sick or wounded. Plus, we have another problem."

"Of course," Rissa said, "there's always another problem. What is it?"

"These mountains were formed by a volcano," the boy said. "It sleeps for now, but if the dragon grows angry, and its breath warms the upper mountains too much …"

"The volcano may awaken," the girl continued, "and then none of us will survive it."

"Swell," Rissa said. "No pressure."

"Can you get us close to them?" Rachel asked.

"Yes, we will help you get to your friend and remove the danger to the Mountains of the Frozen Sky," the leader said, "but you should be armed." He nodded to several of the others, and they hurried off to a side tunnel off the main cavern. In a moment, they returned carrying an armful of short swords and scabbards in which to carry the swords.

"It is a very large dragon," the leader said, "and it doesn't listen to us. It seems unable to even hear us, though Guardians can talk to any creature of the Realm. If it attacks, you will need to defend yourselves if you are to save your friend."

Shaylee took the razor-sharp sword nervously. She didn't like the idea of hurting anything, but as she tied the scabbard around her waist, she knew that she'd do it if that's what it took to save Kaida.

"OK, we're ready," Rissa said when each of the girls had her sword in place. "When do we leave?"

CHAPTER SEVEN
Scaling the Mountains of the Frozen Sky

"You should wear this," said one of the tall, dark-eyed Guardians as he handed Shaylee an odd pair of goggles. They appeared to be carved from wood with slits cut into the wooden "lens" so the wearer could see.

"Thank you," she said. "What do they do?"

"The sun on the ice will burn your eyes," the Guardian boy said. "These will cut the glare so the ice doesn't blind you."

Shaylee slipped them over her head and giggled. "I feel like a fly."

The boy smiled and touched the soft trim on the hood of her coat. "You look more like a seal."

"I guess a seal is better than a fly," Shaylee said. She smiled at the boy. "What's your name?"

"Frost," he said.

"Thank you, Frost," she said.

The Ice Guardians changed smoothly back into massive

polar bears, and the girls climbed onto their backs. Shaylee had watched her new friend Frost grow into the hulking bear, and she kept his kind face in mind as the big bear lumbered over to her and bowed.

This time, Shaylee used a smooth rock bench from inside the cavern to help her reach the bear's back, so she didn't have to be helped up by her friends.

In their special cold-weather clothing, the vicious cold outside the cavern only nipped their faces. They sat upright for a while, looking around as the bears ambled across the smooth, thick ice. In places, huge spikes of ice rose above the level ground. The wind had battered these tall spikes into twisted shapes like pale blue-white sculptures. Shaylee found them beautiful and a little creepy at the same time.

The huge bears covered ground at an amazing rate. The ice that they were traveling across soon changed its angle from almost level and began to ascend upward. They were climbing the ice mountain. The razor-sharp claws of the bears dug in to gain traction as they continued upward.

Ice crystals froze on Shaylee's lashes behind her wooden goggles. She couldn't even feel her nose, and when the wind blew tiny crystals against her cheeks, it felt like something was slicing into her skin. She leaned forward and buried her face in Frost's thick fur; immediately her face felt warm again.

The bear seemed to give off an amazing amount of heat, and Shaylee felt much more comfortable as she snuggled closer. She closed her eyes and rode for a while without looking up. She imagined riding the huge bear at home, maybe to her dance class. Then she giggled as she pictured her dance teacher's reaction to a polar bear striding into the studio with her on its back.

While she was riding on the huge bear's back, it was hard to imagine that she would be afraid of anything. Then she heard someone shout, "Dismount! Everyone off the bears!" Shaylee recognized Rachel's voice. She felt Frost lower himself as close as he could to the ice, and Shaylee slipped off.

The huge bear immediately began pushing her, nearly knocking her off her feet in his haste to move her. She looked in the direction he pushed, but her goggles had been knocked crooked; she could hardly see anything. Still, he gave her another shove, and she felt herself plow into someone.

"Ouch," Rissa said. "That was my foot."

"Get as close as you can to the wall," Rachel yelled.

The girls pressed against the wall, and the bears pressed against them. With her ear so close to the ice wall of the mountain, Shaylee heard a deep rumble. "Is that the dragon?" she asked.

"No," Aly said, "avalanche."

And then the avalanche was upon them. Snow and ice and rocks roared past. Chunks and shards slammed the huge Guardians. Once Shaylee heard a deep throated yelp, and she knew the bears weren't immune to the buffeting. "Oh, please be OK, Frost," she whispered.

It seemed the rumble and crash went on forever. Finally, Aly said, "It's done."

Rachel must have passed on her message because the

bears began to ease away from the girls. "Is everyone OK?" Rachel asked.

"I'm fine," Shaylee said.

"Me too," Aly added.

"I think I'll have some bruises," Rissa said, "but nothing's broken."

Then Marisol spoke, her voice high and strained. "I turned my ankle. It feels like it might be swelling."

Rachel turned and laid a hand on the closest Guardian, passing on the information. The bear reared up on its hind legs and transformed into a boy; he was the leader of the Guardians. He stepped closer to the girls and knelt in front of Marisol.

"I will need to remove your boot," he said quietly. "It will hurt."

Marisol nodded, her dark eyes huge. Shaylee took her friend's hand and gave it a squeeze.

The Guardian gently unlaced the boot and slid it off smoothly. Marisol gasped with the pain and gripped Shaylee's hand tightly enough to make it hurt. Then the boy wrapped his long dark fingers around the swollen ankle and closed his eyes. "It isn't broken," he said. "I can help some, but you'll need to be careful. Perhaps you should go back to the cavern."

Marisol shook her head. "I need to help Kaida."

The boy nodded. "You are very brave, Princess of the Living Waters." Then he closed his eyes, and Shaylee gasped as his hands and Marisol's ankle began to glow.

"Oh, that feels so warm," Marisol said, smiling through tears.

The boy took his hands away and slipped Marisol's boot back on. "You can walk, but it will be weak for a time."

Marisol nodded. "I'll be careful." She reached out and laid a hand on the older boy's arm. "I don't even know your name."

The boy smiled. "Storm."

"Thank you, Storm."

The boy nodded as he tied the laces on Marisol's boot. "We should continue. We will be there soon." He backed away from the girls and changed back into his bear form. Then the girls climbed back on their bears.

"Frost, is that you?" Shaylee asked, looking into the black eyes of the bear that approached her. The bear nodded its shaggy head before crouching next to the nearest ice outcropping where Shaylee could climb back on.

The group headed back along the mountain trail. In places, the avalanche had chipped away at the edge of the trail, making it treacherous for the bears. Shaylee could hear the grinding of their claws against the ice as they moved slowly through the narrow gaps. Once, she peeked over the side of the bear and bit back a scream at the sheer drop that stretched below her. The bear clearly had only inches to spare on the narrow trail. After that, she buried her face in Frost's fur for a while.

She jerked her head up as she heard Rachel shout again. "There's a gap ahead!" she yelled. "The bears say they can jump it, but we'll have to hang on tight."

"Terrific," Rissa said.

Shaylee pressed herself tightly against the bear's back, reaching her fingers deeply into his fur. She waited, her heart pounding. When it was their turn, she felt the muscles bunch under the bear's skin as he prepared. Then he raced ahead, faster than she would have guessed possible. They launched into the air. Then in an instant, she felt the bear slam into solid ground. The force knocked Shaylee sideways, but she hung on and quickly shifted back into place. Frost hurried out of the way so the last bear could make the jump.

Then without more discussion, they continued on. Shaylee thought about the time her brothers had teased her because she didn't want to go on the scariest rides at the fair. After this trip up the mountain, she was pretty sure the fair wouldn't have much that could even make her blink. She hoped the jump was their last roadblock.

She should have wished harder.

The bears came to a halt, and Rachel called out again, "Everyone off. We've got a problem."

Shaylee slipped off Frost, giving her new friend a pat before she walked to where the other girls were gathering. When she reached them, she saw the problem. A massive chasm lay between them and a nearby peak.

"Storm says the dragon cave is not far," Rachel said, "but it's on that side. Either the avalanche triggered an opening between the mountains, or the opening triggered the avalanche. It's possible this is a sign that the volcano is waking up. Either way, the bears can't jump that."

"No surprise," Rissa said. "They'd need wings."

"We need some kind of bridge," Aly said, "but there are no plants here, nothing for me to work with. I can't help."

"Well, if dancing can make us fly, I haven't mastered that yet," Shaylee said.

"I could try a spell, I guess," Rissa said, "if you guys had some idea of what I should be rhyming—maybe pushing the mountains back together?"

"That might cause more problems than it solves," Aly said. "I sense the earth is very unstable. Such a force as that could wake the volcano."

"I might have an answer," Marisol said.

The girls turned to look at her.

"All this ice," she said, "it's just frozen water. I can make it move, I think. I believe I could make a bridge."

"That's probably our best bet," Rachel said, and the others agreed.

"Everyone should step away from the edge; I need as much ice as I can get," Marisol said.

Rachel passed along their friend's plan to the bears, and the whole group backed away from the edge. Shaylee found Frost had moved closer to her as if to shield her from anything that might happen. "I'll be OK," she told him.

Marisol stood near the edge of the jagged cliff and closed her eyes. Across the chasm, the ice seemed to melt away from the stone underneath in a rush. The water flowed quickly to the edge, but instead of obeying gravity and plunging into the chasm, the water stretched defiantly against gravity, reaching for the far edge where the girls stood.

As it stretched, it froze. More water traveled the length of the frozen span to stretch still farther and freeze. The cliffs near where the girls stood began to melt and flow toward the edge on their side. The water avoided Marisol, dividing to flow around her as if she were a rock in a river. The water reached out to touch the frozen span from the other side. It flowed along the span, freezing as it went to thicken the narrow ice bridge. More water moved on either side, and the bridge grew thicker and stronger.

Then Marisol staggered back, opening her eyes as she raised a shaking hand to her head. "That's all I can do."

Storm walked close to the long ice bridge and peered off the side. Then he turned and changed smoothly into a boy. "I believe we will be too heavy for the bridge unless we walk as people," he said. "We will not be able to carry you."

"We can walk it," Rissa said.

"The wind is very strong," Storm said, as the rest of the bears changed into young people. "It will not be easy. You should use your sword as a staff to help you with the crossing. We should walk interspersed so we can help if you have trouble."

"Thank you," Rachel said.

"I'll go first," Marisol said. "I made it, I should test it."

Storm shook his head. "Your ankle is weak. I am not certain you should cross at all."

Marisol looked at him sharply, her dark eyes flashing. "My friend is on that mountain. I'd like to see you try to keep me from going over there to help."

Storm glared at her for a moment, and then he smiled. "You are very brave. I will go with you. But you must hold my hand."

Marisol smiled a little. "I can live with that."

"We will cross two at a time," Storm called out. "Guardians, find your princess. You will cross with them. When one group reaches the other side, the next will go." He held out his hand to Marisol. "Are you ready, Princess?"

"Absolutely," Marisol said, taking his hand.

Just before they stepped out on the ice bridge, Marisol pulled her sword from the scabbard to use as a staff. Then Storm stepped out, and Marisol followed. He paused a moment, closing his eyes and just his feet changed. The boots seemed to vanish as fur and claws appeared, digging into the ice.

The two crossed slowly, and Shaylee could see how the wind pushed and tugged at them. Marisol crowded close to the Guardian boy, but still the wind nearly knocked them from their feet several times.

"I don't know if they can make it," Shaylee whispered. She hoped the wind didn't grow stronger in the center of the bridge where neither mountain shielded them.

"I have to do something about that wind," Rissa said. The girls quickly agreed, and even the Guardians nodded, clearly afraid for their leader. Rissa took a deep breath and called out,

Quiet wind, blow no more.

Stop your push and stop your roar.

The shriek and howl of the wind, which had become a constant background to every moment since they'd reached the shore, now simply stopped. The silence was more still than Shaylee would have thought possible. She could hear the breathing of her friends around her.

Instantly Storm and Marisol picked up their pace and crossed the rest of the bridge without incident.

A bright-eyed Guardian girl took Rachel's hand as they stepped onto the bridge.

"Go quickly," Rissa warned. "I'm not sure how long my spell can keep back something as big as this wind."

Rachel nodded, and they walked quickly across the span. Then another Guardian girl and Aly hurried across. Shaylee could feel her heart pounding as their turn grew closer. She was grateful the wind had stopped, but the bridge still looked long and fragile over the endless drop of the chasm.

"Do you want to go next?" Rissa asked.

Shaylee shook her head. "You go. I'm going to try some deep breathing. It helps with stage fright." She smiled a little. "Maybe it can help with plummeting-to-your-death fright."

Rissa laughed. "Now you sound like me." She took the hand of the Guardian boy beside her, and they headed across the bridge.

"Don't be afraid," Frost said in Shaylee's ear, making her jump. "I will not let you fall."

Shaylee smiled at him. "And who is going to keep you from falling?"

He smiled back. "You. And very sharp claws."

Rissa hopped off the bridge on the other side and waved back at Shaylee. Frost gave Shaylee one last encouraging smile and then stepped out onto the bridge. Instantly his feet transformed into the clawed paws of a polar bear. Shaylee drew her sword to use as a staff and stepped onto the bridge.

Shaylee knew better than to look down, but even without looking at her feet, she could feel the vastness of the chasm under her. She concentrated on carefully placing her feet to keep herself balanced. Her dance training had taught her about moving while always being aware of your balance. The narrow bridge actually seemed plenty wide when she concentrated on her footing instead of what lay below it.

As they reached the middle of the bridge, Shaylee had lost most of her fear. Then she felt a puff of wind against her cheek.

"Hurry!" Rissa shouted from the other side. "The wind is coming back. I can't hold it!"

Frost's grip on her hand tightened as he moved more quickly. Shaylee walked as fast as she dared. Another gust of wind knocked her several steps to the side, and the thin ice crumbled under one foot. Shaylee felt her balance shift, but Frost pulled her ahead. "We can make it!" he shouted as the howl of the wind returned. "It's not much farther."

The bridge widened as it grew closer to the far cliff

edge, but the wind blew harder. Another hard gust nearly knocked Shaylee off her feet, and again Frost caught her. "Sheath your sword," he shouted. "Climb onto my back."

She moved quickly to obey and clung to the boy. He hunched down as if to make a smaller target for the wind and lifted Shaylee off her feet as she held onto him. Then he transformed right on the narrow bridge. He filled out and became the bear again.

Shaylee held on tightly to his thick fur. He moved swiftly across the ice bridge, but Shaylee now heard ominous cracks and groans from the ice below them. Shaylee buried her face in Frost's fur. Then she felt his muscles bunch, and the bear leaped.

The bridge below them seemed to explode from the force of the bear's jump. It rained down into the chasm below. But Frost landed hard on the cliff edge. Instantly, hands grabbed at him and Shaylee, hauling them clear of the dangerous edge. They'd made it.

Shaylee opened her eyes and found herself looking into Rissa's smiling face. "Now for the easy part," her friend said. "We just have to rescue a princess from a dragon!"

CHAPTER EIGHT
Taming the Dragon

Shaylee looked around and spotted a polar bear climbing heavily to his feet. "Frost?" she called, "Are you all right?"

The bear transformed back into a boy, and Shaylee gasped when she saw a raw scrape on the side of his face. He smiled. "I will be fine. I've gotten more scrapes than this just wrestling with my brother." He grinned toward Storm.

"But this was for a better cause," Storm said. "Good job."

The others patted Frost on the back and congratulated him. After just a moment of the well wishing, Storm held up a hand. "We must move on. We cannot be out in the open after dark. The cold will freeze us to the very core."

The group headed along a narrow path that wove away from them around the mountain. "That cave is not far now," Storm whispered.

Shaylee wasn't sure if she was glad or terrified to know they were almost there. She was as tired as she'd ever been.

She'd once thought dance camp was the biggest workout she'd ever get, but being a princess was turning out to be a lot more challenging. When she'd played princess as a little girl, there hadn't been any death-defying leaps on the backs of polar bears.

The cold made the bones in her face ache. At least much of the blowing ice was blocked as they walked close to the mountainside. The group crept forward now as quietly as possible. Up ahead, Shaylee could see the shadows that signaled an opening in the side of the mountain. Was that the dragon's cave?

Storm waited until everyone had gathered in front of the cave entrance, and then together they walked in. Like the Guardian's cave, this one wasn't really dark inside. More of the strangely glowing crystals were embedded in the walls. Shaylee wondered if that meant the crystals just occurred naturally here, or if this cavern had once been lived in.

The passageway was huge with the ceiling of the cavern towering far above their heads. The width allowed them to walk five across without hitting the walls. Somehow the vastness surprised Shaylee, even though she knew it had to be big if a whole dragon had come inside.

Then she realized her face was beginning to feel warm again. The cavern was growing warmer. Storm turned to them and silently mouthed, "Dragon."

The passage turned sharply, and they saw they had reached the cavern's end. The final chamber was huge, and the walls were so encrusted with the glowing crystals that it was as bright as daylight. The walls were lined with the same kind of carved-rock benches and shelves they'd seen in the Guardian's cave, but the crystals were so abundant that everything either sparkled or glowed.

In the center of the cavern, Kaida's dragon lay sleeping, curled up. Clearly he'd continued to grow as they'd flown away; his head alone was as big as two of the Guardian bears.

The golden thread Kaida had used to outline the blues and greens of the dragon in the picture now caused every scale to sparkle when hit by light. The huge wings lay folded tightly against the creature's back. His eyes were closed, and Shaylee could see golden eyelashes against the dragon's scaly cheeks.

The long blue-green tail curled around the creature. In one of the crooks of the dragon's tail, Kaida lay sleeping. Marisol gasped and took a step toward her friend. Storm reached out and caught her arm. "This is how we used to find the Sky Warriors. "We cannot awaken her, and we do not want to awaken the dragon."

"Do you think the sleep could be magical?" Aly asked.

"We simply do not know," Storm said.

"Well, we didn't come all this way to leave her behind," Rissa said. "We have to try to wake her up."

She strode over to the dragon with Marisol right by her side. Rachel and Aly followed. The thought of getting any closer to the massive dragon made Shaylee feel shaky inside, but she took a deep breath and followed her friends.

They got as close to Kaida as possible without touching the dragon, and Marisol called out in a whisper, "Kaida!"

Their friend didn't move.

She called again a bit louder. Still neither the girl nor the dragon twitched. Finally, Marisol shouted, but still they slept. The princesses shouted together, their voices filling the cavern, but the dragon and girl slept. "We're going to have to touch her," Rissa said, and she stepped up on the dragon's tail. The tail twitched, sending Rissa flying backward, and she landed on her rear on the cavern floor.

Marisol and Aly ran to their friend. Shaylee turned to look at the dragon's face for signs of wakening. But the creature's eyes stayed closed. "It must have been some kind of reflex," Rachel said.

"Great," Rissa said as her friends hauled her to her feet. "But that's one wild ride."

Shaylee took a deep breath. "I could try. I'm lighter, and I might not trigger the reflex. Plus, I've been training to keep my balance since I was four years old. Balance is half of what dancing is all about."

The girls looked at one another. They didn't like the idea but didn't really see another option. "No," a voice said firmly behind them. "That is too dangerous."

They turned to see that Frost had stepped up to join them. His brother followed.

"There's no choice," Shaylee said. "We have to wake her up."

"One of us should go," Frost said.

"Right, 'cause you guys are so wispy and light," Rissa responded.

"It's unacceptable for the princess to go!" Frost's face darkened, but his brother took his arm gently.

"They are right," Storm said.

"You saw what the beast did," Frost responded. "She could get hurt."

"The princess is brave," Storm answered. "We need to be brave with her. And we can move close to catch her if she should take flight." He said this last part with a small smile.

"That would be good," Shaylee said. She finally turned and began unlacing her boots. "It will be easier for me to stay on the slippery surface barefoot. And it's warm in here." She stepped up carefully onto the long tail. The dragon's scales shone like polished metal and were as slippery as they looked.

When Shaylee put her weight on her foot to step up, the tale shifted slightly in the smallest twitch, but it did not fling the girl as it had Rissa. With each step Shaylee took, a fresh ripple ran along the dragon's skin. She concentrated on keeping her weight carefully balanced so she could adjust to each twitch and ripple without falling. She knew the irritation might eventually make the tail really jump, so she had to hurry.

The dragon's tail was warm under her feet like walking on the sidewalk on a sunny day in spring. Finally, she reached the coil where Kaida lay sleeping. Shaylee crouched next to her friend. She shook the sleeping girl gently, then a bit harder. "Kaida!"

Kaida opened her eyes and blinked. "Shaylee?" she said, and then she smiled. "I was having the strangest dream."

"Well, we're having a pretty strange awake time," Shaylee said. "Come on, we have to get out of here."

Kaida sat up and looked around. "Oh, right. Now I remember. How did you get here?"

"We had a lot of help," Shaylee said. "But we can tell you all about it as soon as we get out of here."

The small girl struggled to haul her taller friend to her feet. Kaida ran her hand over her face as she stood. "Feeling a little wobbly," she said.

"We think you might have been under some kind of magic spell," Shaylee said. She hauled Kaida across the first coil of tail. Kaida kept blinking and weaving a little, making it hard for Shaylee to keep her footing. At least the tail had stopped trembling.

"I'm so sleepy," Kaida said. "Maybe I could just have a little nap?"

"No," Shaylee snapped. "Wake up." She pinched Kaida hard on the arm and her friend jumped.

"Ouch, that hurt," Kaida said, but her eyes cleared a bit.

"Um, Shaylee," Rissa called. "You better hurry. I think the dragon is waking up."

Kaida was able to stay on her feet better for several steps, and then her eyes seemed to grow heavy again. Shaylee gave her another hard pinch, muttering, "Sorry about that."

Kaida's eyes snapped open again, and she pulled her arm out of Shaylee's hands. "Stop that!"

"We have to get off of here," Shaylee said.

The dragon's tail moved in a slow purposeful roll. The girls jumped off, landing on the cavern floor near their friends. The dragon's head turned toward them, and its eyes narrowed as it looked at Kaida rubbing her sore arm.

"Guardians," Storm called, "change!" In a moment, the girls were surrounded by the bears. The sudden change seemed to upset the dragon still more. It stood, turning to face the bears squarely. Then it roared.

The sound made the cavern rumble and groan. Shaylee slammed her hands over her aching ears. "I think we made it mad," she said.

The dragon dipped its head closer to the bears and roared again. One of the huge bears slashed at the dragon's snout with its clawed paws. The dragon jerked back slightly then snapped at the bear. More of the bears joined the fight, striking at the dragon in a half dozen places.

"We have to help," Rachel called as she pulled out her sword. "The dragon's too big for them." The other girls pulled their swords and rushed at the huge creature.

With amazing speed, Kaida ran ahead and grabbed the sword from Marisol's hand. Then she jumped lightly up on the dragon's head. "Stop!" she yelled. "Leave him alone." She swung her sword at the nearest bear, just missing its slashing paws.

"Hey," Rissa yelled back, "we're on your side."

"Then leave him alone!" Kaida demanded. "Leave him alone and back off!"

The bears obeyed immediately, backing away from the huge dragon. The dragon seemed to calm at once. It held its head still as Kaida looked down on her friends. "The dragon thought you were attacking me. He's not a monster."

"He kidnapped you," Marisol said.

"It was a misunderstanding," Kaida said. "He's good. Really." She jumped lightly from the dragon's head to the floor of the cavern. "I would have come back, but while I was getting used to communicating with him, we fell asleep."

"I think there must be some kind of spell on this cavern," Rissa said.

Kaida nodded. "I'm already feeling a little sleepy again." Then she pointed at Shaylee. "But no pinching."

"We should get out of here," Rissa said.

Several of the Guardians pulled warm clothing out of the packs they carried, and Kaida was soon dressed warm enough to go outside. By the time they had her bundled into the clothes, she was already blinking and swaying. The dragon also blinked, his head dipping as he scrambled unsteadily to his feet. The Guardians all gave the swaying dragon plenty of room, in case he staggered or fell. The dragon clearly would not allow Kaida far from his sight, even if every movement was a struggle.

"I don't know why it only affects Kaida and the dragon," Marisol said. "I feel fine."

"I have a theory," Storm said. "But we should get outside. I will explain there."

As the second tallest of the girls, Marisol supported Kaida on one side as their friend stumbled toward the cave opening. Once outside, the icy wind hit them like a hammer. Any sign of sleepiness quickly passed.

The dragon settled just inside the cavern entrance as the trail wasn't wide enough for both the dragon and the people. He thrust his head out of the cavern and stopped blinking sleepily.

"I believe the cavern has been enchanted to put Sky Warriors to sleep. It is leftover magic from the war," Storm said.

"What war?" Kaida said.

"That is a very long story, and this is no place for storytelling," the boy pointed at the sky. "It will be dark soon. We could spend the night in this cavern, and climb down in the morning, but we need to get the dragon off the mountain. Can you send it away?"

Kaida shook her head. "I don't think he would leave me, but we could ride him."

"You mean fly?" Shaylee squeaked. "On the dragon?"

"Yes," Kaida said. "It's magnificent. And warm."

"I don't think the Folk in the village would like to see the dragon again," Rachel said. "They were pretty freaked out."

"I've been thinking about that," Rissa said. "I think I could possibly do a spell to put him back in the picture. Then if you wrapped it up, he should stay there."

Kaida patted the dragon's nose. "I hate to put him back," she said. "I was getting kind of attached."

"I know your dad likes adventurous living," Marisol said, "but there is no way he'd let you keep this pet."

"Do you think I could keep the picture?" Kaida asked. "Then if we needed him sometime when we're here, we could bring him out."

Shaylee giggled. "I'm pretty sure Spindlethorne does *not* want the picture back."

"I have an idea," Marisol said. She walked back into the cavern and put her hand on the ice-covered wall near one of the glowing crystals. The ice on the wall melted, and the crystal tumbled down into her hands. "You could give this to Spindlethorne. It seems like a useful thing. He could use it like a flashlight."

Kaida nodded and slipped the crystal into her pocket. "OK, are we ready to go?"

The girls turned to the Guardians. "Do you want us to give you a lift back down the mountain?" Rachel asked.

Storm shook his head. "There is another path that should be open. It is longer, but we are in no hurry. We'll sleep here in the cavern through the cold night and go home in the morning." Then he bowed slightly, and the other Guardians did as well. "We are honored to have met the princesses."

"And we are very grateful for your help," Marisol said.

"We will miss you," Frost said, his eyes on Shaylee.

Shaylee felt her cheeks grow warm. "I'll miss you too. Thanks for saving my life."

"Thank you for making my life more interesting," Frost said. He took her hand and gave it a slight squeeze. Then all the Guardians stepped out of the way so the dragon could take off once the princesses were on its back.

The dragon laid his head flat on the ground, and Kaida jumped lightly upon it. "It's easiest to ride on his neck now that he's so big," Kaida said. "It's only about as broad as a horse's back, and there are short spines to hold onto."

"Spines sound painful," Rissa said.

Kaida laughed. "It will make you tough."

The dragon held completely still as the girls walked across his neck and took spots between his spines, which turned out to feel a lot like the back fins of the dolphins. Shaylee thought about the amazing creatures they'd met on this trip to the Realm of Wellspring.

"Everyone ready?" Kaida called out. "The ride is pretty smooth, but you'll need to hang on."

Each of the girls shouted back, "Ready!"

The dragon stepped carefully out onto the narrow path and spread his wings. Most of his tail was still inside the cavern. The huge wings swept up and down as if warming up, and then the great creature leaped from the cliff.

Shaylee gave a muffled scream at the sudden downward plunge of the dragon. It was like the coldest, scariest roller coaster she'd ever been on. The icy wind rushed by her face. She gripped the dragon's spine so tightly her fingers ached, and still the dragon plunged down farther and farther.

Then the huge creature seemed to catch the wind; the downward plunge turned into an inverted arc, and he began climbing toward the sky. His huge wings beat the air with a roaring swoosh. Finally, the flight settled into a smoother glide, and the dragon circled the top of the mountain.

Looking down, the girls could barely make out the dark gash in the side of the mountain that was the giant cavern. With a final circle, the dragon turned, and they left the Mountains of the Frozen Sky behind as they sailed far above the beautiful waters and headed back toward land.

CHAPTER NINE
The Party at Last

Dusk approached more quickly as they rushed through the sky away from the setting sun. Shaylee peered down at the waves that were well below them. The sun's final rays struck the water and made the surface glow like molten fire.

Rissa leaned forward and spoke close to Shaylee's ear. "I guess Rachel's not the only one with a Realm boyfriend now."

"What are you talking about?" Shaylee asked.

"Well, Frost didn't give my hand a little goodbye squeeze," her friend said.

"He was just being friendly," Shaylee insisted, though her cheeks burned. "After all, he did save my life."

"Right."

Shaylee put a cool hand against her warm cheeks and realized she was going to know exactly what it was like to get all the teasing her friends had been giving Rachel. She smiled. Actually, it was worth it. Then she realized

93

they weren't likely to have any reason for going back to the cold, barren mountains. She easily might not ever see the dark-eyed shape changer again.

Though in Wellspring, you never really knew.

Shaylee's thoughts were so occupied with her new friend that the trip over the sea seemed to take only minutes. Then they were soaring over the trees before reaching the village. The large meadow was still deserted as the dragon circled it in slow even sweeps before landing.

The girls slipped from his neck and began searching for the picture that had brought the dragon to the Realm. "There's so much stuff scattered everywhere," Rachel said, "and we're losing the light."

Kaida looked around and saw torches had been placed on long poles throughout the field. Obviously the party had been meant to last into the evening. As she pointed at each torch, it burst into flames, casting a pool of light under it. Soon the field was softly lit, and the searching went faster.

As they hunted through the wreckage, a few of the Meadow Folk ventured out of the side streets. They walked hesitantly, at first, their eyes fixed on the enormous dragon. But the dragon lay on the ground quietly with its eyes closed as Kaida scratched his snout. Soon more and more of the Folk stepped out and asked the princesses what they were searching for. As soon as they found out, they joined in the hunt.

"I'm glad to see you back," Honeyglow said to Shaylee when the golden-haired Guardian joined the hunt. "I was a little bit worried."

"I was a whole lot worried," Shaylee said with a smile, "but it was fantastic really." Then she looked around them at the growing crowd of people joining the hunt. "Are they mad at us?"

Honeyglow shook her head. "They love you. You're their princess. Plus, we've never had such an exciting Feast Cycle Celebration in all of the history of the Folk. They will tell this story forever. And the Folk love stories."

Shaylee smiled. "And they don't even know the best parts."

"You should tell them."

"I'll leave that to Rissa," Shaylee said. "She's better with words."

Shaylee spotted something dangling from one of the small trees that dotted the field at wildly spaced intervals. All of the trees were full of blossoms. At the base of each one was a small bench carved with more flowers. This particular tree bloomed with more than flowers. Something rectangular dangled from a high branch, making a dark outline against the sky. "That might be it," Shaylee said. "I'm going to climb up."

"Be careful," Honeyglow whispered.

Shaylee smiled. At one time she'd been scared of climbing trees, but now the small tree seemed as safe as a ladder. She climbed quickly and pulled the bit of debris from the branch.

She slipped back down before looking clearly at it. It was definitely the cross-stitch picture. The frame was broken, and the dark blue cross-stitch cloth looked ink black in the dim light. Still, the thin golden thread that had formed a design around the dragon glistened.

"I found it!" Shaylee shouted.

The princesses gathered around the picture. Kaida took it and carefully pulled off the broken bits of frame.

"Do you want me to try the spell now?" Rissa asked.

"I want to try something else first," Kaida said. She carried the soft fabric over to the dragon. She rubbed the huge creature's scaly snout, and then whispered in its ear. The dragon chuffed softly.

It stood up, curling its long neck to gently circle Kaida. Then, it began to shrink. Kaida kept a gentle hand on it until the dragon shrank to the size of a cat. Then it began to beat its wings, lifting it lightly into the air as it continued to shrink. It opened its mouth wide and roared, sounding more like the bark of a small dog than the ground-shaking sound it had made in the cavern.

Finally, when the dragon had shrunk to the size of a bird, it circled Kaida's head once in a playful swoop before darting back into the picture. Kaida reached up to wipe a tear from her eye and then gently rolled up the cross-stitch cloth.

The crowd that had gradually filled the meadow cheered. Spindlethorne walked over to Kaida and said, "Thank you, Princess, for a most exciting day."

"Would you mind," Kaida said, "if I gave you this gift instead?" She reached into her coat pocket and handed over the glowing crystal. "It seems like a more useful present."

Spindlethorne sighed in relief. "Yes, Princess, I am

grateful for this gift. The dragon should stay with his master."

The villagers closest to the princesses laughed at the exchange. Then everyone began scurrying around the meadow. Tables filled with food were carried out. A group of musicians took up a place on what was left of the gift platform and began playing cheery tunes, and the Folk began to dance.

All the girls shucked off the thick coats that had kept them cozy on the ice-covered mountains. They were entirely too warm for dancing in the beautiful meadow. The few unbroken gifts were gathered and exchanged. Surprisingly all of the girls' presents had survived, and a few brave Folk stepped forward to receive them nervously.

Aly's gift was a thick wooden barrette that she'd painted with flowering vines. The woman who received it was the head gardener for the village. She laughed with delight as she clipped the barrette into her thick white hair, and the flowers burst forth from the barrette, trailing vines and blooms down the woman's back. "Oh, Princess," the gardener gasped, "it is so lovely."

In return, she had given Aly a bag filled with seeds from the Realm. "I don't know how our flowers will look in your world," the woman said, "but I hope they bring much beauty for you."

Aly's eyes were shiny with happiness. "Thank you," she said. "I'll plant them as soon as I get home."

Rissa's gift of the calligraphy poem was given to the

head musician. He immediately held up the beautifully written parchment and began to sing the poem about a cat chasing mice. The stenciled cats leaped from the paper and rubbed against his legs. "Thank you, Princess," he said with a grin. "I've had a problem with mice nibbling the strings of our instruments. I think that problem is solved."

In return, he gave Rissa a small box filled with songs. When she opened the box, beautiful, rich music poured out. "I love it," she said.

Marisol's gift was a large conch shell that she'd painted with Aly's help, so that the outside showed a seashore at sunset. When the young girl who received it tipped the shell, water poured out. The girl clapped her hand in delight. In return, she gave Marisol an intricately carved hair comb.

"You just imagine how you would like your hair to look," the girl said. "Then begin combing, and it will make the style for you."

Marisol ran the comb through her hair a few times, and the thick dark waves quickly wrapped themselves into a beautiful updo with a few trailing curls. "Oh, this is perfect!"

After the gift giving, the girls were pulled into the dance. Laughing, the girls tried to match the intricate steps of the group dances and often ended up in a giggling pile, which seemed to delight the villagers.

Shaylee joined dance after dance before she finally had to step away to catch her breath. She watched her friends for a moment and then noticed Rachel standing a bit apart, sipping from a cup. Shaylee thought her friend looked sad and walked over to join her.

"Are you OK?" Shaylee asked.

Rachel shrugged and then leaned closer to whisper. "Don't tell anyone—and don't laugh. I don't want to be teased. I guess I really hoped I'd get to see Fleet."

"I'm not going to laugh," Shaylee said. "I think I know how you feel. I don't know if I'll ever see Frost again. I mean, we're not really going to spend a lot of time up on the icy mountain."

Rachel nodded, and then she turned to Shaylee with a small smile. "Still, we never really know, do we? This place is full of surprises. Eventually I want to hear about that war that Storm mentioned. So maybe we'll go back for a little storytelling session."

"Maybe." Shaylee stretched and looked back at the happy dancers. "But for now, I think I have one more dance in me before we go home. What about you?"

Rachel nodded, and they ran back to join the group. Soon the girls began saying their goodbyes to their new friends and the old friends they were revisiting. Eidermoss gave each of the princesses a hug and begged them to come back soon.

The princesses joined hands and pictured the clothes they'd worn before stepping through the portal. Shaylee smiled as she found it almost hard to remember; much had happened since that moment. It seemed as though they'd been in the Realm for months instead of only a day.

When they finally had their clothes sorted out, they

opened the portal and stepped through. The members of the Folk called out goodbyes until the portal finally closed.

"I don't know about everyone else," Shaylee said, "but I need a nap."

"Really?" Kaida responded. "I feel very well rested."

"Sure, you slept through the whole adventure," Marisol said, laughing as she gave Kaida a friendly shove. "It's too bad too. You would have made a great mermaid."

"Mermaid!" Kaida repeated in horror. "I really don't think I'm the mermaid type."

"Especially with all the other mermaids giggling and draping you with pearls," Rissa said. "You'd look so dainty."

Kaida shuddered. "Maybe I'm glad I slept through that."

"You would have liked the ice bridge," Rissa said. "It was terrifying, especially when Shaylee's new boyfriend had to save her life by jumping from the falling ice."

"He's not my boyfriend," Shaylee snapped.

Kaida walked over and hopped up to sit on the table. "You'll have to tell me all about it."

Rissa yawned widely. "Not from me. I'm with Shaylee on this one. I need a nap."

The yawning quickly grew contagious, and the girls begged off sharing the story so they could go home and rest. Then Rissa called out, "Don't forget to write down your account of this adventure while it's still fresh in your head."

All the girls groaned at that. More homework.

As they drifted toward the door, Kaida said, "Next time

I am definitely not missing out on all the excitement."

"Next time, maybe you won't be the cause of it," Rissa replied.

"Hey, if Rachel had just kept her magical animal paws off my gift, none of this would have happened," Kaida said with a smile.

"Well whose bright idea was it to stitch a ferocious dragon?" Rachel shot back. "Next time try something cute and harmless—like a bunny." She gave Kaida a friendly hug and they all headed out the door.

They never knew who might be the cause of the excitement. In the Realm of Wellspring, the only sure thing was that the adventure would be like nothing they could imagine, and that was starting to suit Shaylee just fine.

The End

Don't miss
the next book in this
exciting adventure series!

Log on to
AnniesCraftStore.com/Enchanted
to sign up for new release alerts,
AND you'll get a special coupon
for **15% OFF** your next purchase
with **Annie's!**